Like Me, For Me

Also by Isabella Juanita Lyn
Everything I Couldn't Say
A Strangled Heart

Like Me, For Me

Isabella Juanita Lyn

ISBN: 978-0-6486490-9-0 (eBook) 978-0-6486490-8-3 (paperback)

First Edition: March 2025

 A catalogue record for this book is available from the National Library of Australia

A flower always blooms after
wilting

Period

1

Sometimes I wished

That photo day didn't exist,
that I didn't feel the pressure to be pretty,
that our photos weren't the be all, end all.

I hated this

What was the reason for annual photos
where no one's prepared, happy, excited...
What was the reason for the photos we dreaded,
what was the reason for the photos we cherished,
what was the reason for the photos we hated?

These photos weren't only a memory in time.
They held stronger promise than what met the eye,
acting like a jigsaw holding together
a small part of our self-worth
before it came crashing down
into further fragmented pieces of true beauty.

I hated these photos,
the ones made a part of our student identification
and the ones used for our never-ending number of
assemblies.

It was a marker,
not just for us but for them.
To forever remember us in a superficial way,
bounded by academics, extracurriculars, achievements,
social circles, athletics.

The movies and books told us that
high school was a popularity contest.
But the real sea of high school

contained shark cages, trained to wait for their prey,
and willingly sink their teeth
until we're battered, bruised, broken.

Those school photos weren't of moments that mattered,
but they were the symbol of everything that should've.

High school became an institution
that harboured the secrets of the youth,
waiting for the perfect moment
to dismantle, destroy, *demolish* their self-esteem
without ever hearing the blow.

~~I hated these photos~~
~~but I almost wished I didn't.~~

Why was this mandatory?

It was hard to believe anyone benefited
from the school photo days *but* those who clicked the
cameras.
Classes, disrupted and entangled in messes of
imperfection,
students, lined in zigzags arranged by surname,
me, a collage of fragments too far from the melting point
to be whole.

I never liked photo days.

Maybe at one point, I did.

I liked having photos taken,
I liked displaying them on my desk,
I liked having a snapshot of the memory.

But these days, photo days were a bomb
waiting to drop and unmask the way my eyes
were too wide set apart, the way my makeup
lacked the airbrush of magazines, the way my hair
hung lowly on the back of my head
with the one stray strand that never cooperated.

When the flash came, my eyes closed.

Photo defeated.

They made me smile again,
more crooked than the last.
My cheeks feeling the ache,
sinking down and appearing saggy
for such a young age.

Maybe I should've considered cosmetic surgery...

This time, the flash came
and I didn't shut my eyes.
The pain of the burn
reminded me of who I was becoming,
of who I'm meant to be,
 of who I'd almost never be.

In this filtered world,
school photos were a day we
imprinted perfection under our names
for the rest of the year into forever.

Yes, it was an annual occurrence,
but first impressions lasted.

Photo companies continued to benefit from our demise,
their living made from our insecurities
spotlighted into the cruel, soul-crushing world
of popularity, status, gossip.

 They never knew

the behind-the-scenes we hid
from a young age when beauty
became everything but who we were.

No, they never knew...

They never knew
how mandatory school photos
were vices holding us against our will,
punishing us through
our well-being, our self-worth.

Ripping us into pieces of

a jigsaw no one could rebuild.
No one but us.

And most jigsaws were never completed again.

I understood why school photos were mandatory,
the nature of keeping accurate profiles
and updating records without the hassle
of finding out who dyed their hair,
got a fresh tan,
had a glow-up and *whatever else.*

But the mandatory school photo was only one day
out of the whole school year.
Who was to say we wouldn't change?

Who was to say we couldn't go through a new phase?
Who was to say we were stuck in time like our photos in
printed ink?

But the worst part of it all wasn't its frequency
but the urgency it demanded in forever keeping the
pieces apart.

I wanted this day to be over

More than I wanted an exam to never start.
I had no heart, no help, no hope
that this day was going to be good.

My gut churned,
heartbeat spiralling out of control,
and sweat beading around my forehead
while my makeup fought to stay impeccable.

The concealer creased; mascara ran.
Nothing looked perfect on me.
Nothing would ever look perfect on me
no matter
how hard I tried to fit in,
with the pressures of high school, the trauma
of hearing I'd never meet their expectations of "pretty".

I wanted this day to be over before I even woke up.

Insecurities

I hated the way I looked in photos,
the way my hair fell unnaturally,
my smile crooked and forced,
my eyes, small and invisible to the lens.

You told me I was "beautiful"
but you liked photos of supermodels,
and the photos of me burnt to ashes in the fireplace
you kissed me in front of
the night of our first date.
The flames caught sight of the last moment
of pure love, now bokeh moments that

haunted me.

I hated the way my nose was so big
and the way my body wasn't thin enough for you.
To the point I starved myself, exercised until my bones
gave out,
and I was frail but still not "beautiful".

Everything I did to achieve perfection
was considered terrible, rushed, imperfect.
The makeup I wore, the routines I followed,
the countless hours and money I spent to
become the models you effortlessly pursued.

But I still wasn't beautiful to you.

The photo, taken while thoughts
raced miles in my mind around my heart.
I saw you talking to my best friend in line.
We didn't share the same classes
nor were you seen with me in public.

I was never going to be your "beautiful"
but one day I would be.

One day...

Beautiful wasn't beautiful

if done for anyone but you.

I hated the way I looked

But who didn't when told that their whole life?
Who wouldn't hurt when they heard
that they were never enough
their whole life?

Never enough for anyone but them...

Period

2

Flash

For the first time,
the lights blinded me.
They never stunned my smile to stone.
But today, the world around me erupted
a haze of fuzzy spots and white light.

The colour of innocence and peace was dark and guilty.

Forgotten moments

I wished this was a moment I could easily forget
but I knew better than you did
about hearts getting broken.

Memories of us resurfaced when I saw you
but they didn't bring a smile to my face.

These memories of you
held only moments of betrayal,
your lips on my best friend's and
your lock on the door as I waited
outside on dark stormy nights,
watching you pull her in closer

until
       all
              the
                     space
                           was

gonegonegonegonegonegonegonegonegonegonegone.
gonegonegonegonegonegonegonegonegonegonegone.
gonegonegonegonegonegonegonegonegonegonegone.
gonegonegonegonegonegonegonegonegonegonegone.
gonegonegonegonegonegonegonegonegonegonegone.
gonegonegonegonegonegonegonegonegonegonegone.
gonegonegonegonegonegonegonegonegonegonegone.
gonegonegonegonegonegonegonegonegonegonegone.

Was there ever any truth

To "I love you"?

I sometimes wondered if there was truth in those
moments
I called the nuances to our relationship.
The nuances that made us special, made you special,

made me special.

I wanted to believe it was true,
whether for my delusion
or the hope that you cared.

"I love you" wasn't only an expression,
a phrase of gratitude for another person.
"I love you" meant more than a declaration, a confession.

But your "I love you" didn't match any definition,
repeated over and over like the shutter of the camera.
The mechanical movement of the mirror and shutter
blades
cut through your words (~~I love you~~)
                              before they reached my ears.

And the worst part...

It couldn't convince me our love was still here.

But even now I couldn't fool myself with your exposed words.

18

"Love you" didn't mean

What it should have with you.

You broke me

The way you dropped my phone so casually into the
ocean
when I got that call from my guy best friend

and the way you ran over my cat like she meant nothing
from my late father who I'd never see again

and the moment you deleted all those memory backups
when my mother moved to another continent

and the night you stabbed me with a kitchen knife
because you were sick of me.

You broke me.

Messages

They shouldn't have had the power to destroy me

but they did.

As wrong as it was
to snatch your phone from your hand
against your desperate attempt to prove
your innocence,
guilt was an emotion long forgotten.

I gave you my deepest secrets,
held you so highly with trust,
and you repaid me with this?

Did you like me for who I truly was
or was I forever a sculpted beauty in your mind?

Everyone I wanted to prove us to,
to show that we *were* compatible,
that we would have lasted,
meant to be,

were against us.

For the first time in four years,
I gained clarity.

You: The day we became official was the worst.
What was I thinking, asking her?
I must've been on steroids or something...

Best friend: Still couldn't believe you chose her over me.
Like I'm always the better option.
Right?
You love me more, don't you?

You: Of course I do!
She was a mistake,
one I made blindly
but I see plainly how wrong I was
and the missing puzzle piece
is clear as day.

Best friend: She's not even that pretty.
She needed all that makeup
to become friends with me.
She was such a brat,
asking me to do this and that.
I always had to reassure her before
we went out.
EVEN IF IT WAS FOR A WALK!
Like I didn't care if she got sweaty.
She wasn't looking great in the first place.
She was infuriating.
She was selfish.
She was insecure.

How did you put up with her for so long?
Those four years must've been torture for you...
Her makeup skills weren't even that good
even after she started learning and taking classes.
She only wanted reminders
that she was the prettiest girl alive.
When she never even looked pretty.
No wonder she's so clingy...

You: Her makeup looked like trash
every single time anyway.
It's embarrassing going out with her.
Why did I stay with her for so long...
Those four years were terrible.
Should've let her go years before...

Best friend: Exactly!
She never deserved someone like you.
Handsome, charismatic, lit up any room.
She's invisible without you
and too visible with you.
Not to mention, she was so desperate.
She needs to know she's pretty
every
single
day!

You: Getting rid of her was the
best decision I've made

since accidentally getting involved
with her.
But at least I got good money from it all.
Now we can have those fancy dates
I would never take her on, princess.

Best friend: She's so gullible, I love it!

You: She did everything I asked for.
It was almost too easy!

Best friend: Waiting for the day you dump her.
Make it worthwhile babe!

You: Trust me, princess, we were worth the wait!

Her feelings clear as day,
your control apparent,
my heart, in pieces,
chained by undeveloped negatives.

"Babe, I didn't mean to—"

I slammed your phone back into your palm.
I ran, your true feelings and her empty promises
drumming on my heart until I couldn't breathe.

The pieces of my heart cascaded down,
my stomach acid dissolving gratefully.

I wasn't the only incomplete puzzle today.

But I was missing pieces I doubted I'd find again.

Unlike you two.

Broken hearts

I couldn't admit to myself that you didn't love me the
way I loved you.

But my broken heart wasn't tearing apart like paper
under the guise of true love for a beauty
you couldn't even stand on her worst days.

And that was every day.

I couldn't admit to myself that you didn't love me the
way I loved you.

When I would've fought to keep embers burning,
you hid in a darkroom to develop false relationships
with the one I trusted most, and you wanted more.

Broken hearts smelt suspicion.

I couldn't admit to myself that you didn't love me the
way I loved you.

Because what use was there to live with a broken heart
when lies were easier to bear?

Vision untrue

I never wanted to believe you kissed her.
The one girl you compared me to
and the one girl you promised was never prettier than
me.

You: Come on babe, just wear the blue dress.
Your friend looked great in it so you will too.

> *Me: But it's not baggy enough.*
> *Too tight and fitted in all the places–*

You: JUST THROW ON THE DRESS SO WE CAN
LEAVE!

The dress hugged all my curves in the wrong ways,
I felt your disdain rolling off my spine each time
your fingertips brushed my arm to push me slightly
further.

I knew you hated how it looked on me.

I wanted to believe her when she said
your love meant nothing to her,
that there was nothing between you.
I wanted to believe when she said
it wasn't you when I suspected

you were kissing her,
leaving reminders for her,
treating her like the queen she was

and forgetting me in the dirt
of the untamed ovals where balls flew in the air
and players ran wild.

Best friend: Girl, you look nice today...
Maybe consider eating less the next time
we go out.
Then you'll be prettier!

Best friend: I love how you dress so effortlessly.
But maybe try the baggy jeans next time.

Best friend: Is that the high-end makeup you just
bought?
Girl, it's doing a bad job. Your pores are not covered.
Give them to me instead
and leave this to the professionals.
Like me!
Drugstore makeup suited your skin more anyway.

Believing you through backhanded compliments
taught me things I never knew about humanity.
How could someone have been so cruel, so selfish,
so perfectly imperfect?

You told me the things I needed to hear
but you told me more about yourself
than I saw through you in four years.

Best friend or not, the past was in the past
and the present unfolded before my very eyes.

You: Finally dumping her today
but let's meet up before I do, princess.

      Best friend: Always down for a rendezvous!

You're done with me now

               She wanted you

but you wanted her all along.

          and she always had you.

What else were you hiding

When we were dating that you didn't have the heart to
tell me?

Sometimes I questioned if there even was a heart.
Was it beating, keeping you alive,
circulating your oxygen?

What kept you alive if there wasn't?

Were you a filter
manipulating our reality?

Were you a memory card,
repeating the slideshow
crafted and hidden to destroy hearts?

Were you a glitching greenscreen
streaming my life, my relationships
for one you controlled, changing
the green to red,
so I would never be

      out

                    of

                                        line?

Did you have a heart beating in there at all?

I'm not a cardiologist,
but I'm certain it died before we did.

The crash

We burned faster than we crashed.

Where would you have been

If we didn't have school photos today?
Would you have stayed home
or would you have walked the same halls?
Would you have asked me on a date
or would you be kissing her while I was studying?

You: Meet me in the back oval.

Best friend: Got it.

I guess I didn't have to be far
for you to break promises anymore.

Captured moments

They were special, fragments of time
we would cherish for the rest of our lives.
Maybe, maybe not?
We were still highschoolers at day's end,
and the future wasn't set in stone.
But they said, "when you know, you know,"
and that was you.

Until it wasn't.

You didn't want us

You never did,
but I always wanted you.

If only

I didn't see you.

You cancelled our date
because your boss called you in for work.
Who was I to dictate your life?
This was the fifth date you ran from
but at least this one was valid...

You: Hey babe, too busy to hang out later.

You: Babe, cancel tonight, something came up.
Don't ask about it.

You: Don't wait up, not coming over tonight.

You: Too tired, see you at school.

If only I had captured the moment,
would you believe me then?
You wished for me to fall into your lies
as a Pinocchio who loathed when
I thought I looked bad, wanted to cover up,
hated my body for surviving in its hideous form.

I threw on another baggy sweater.
"Take that off, you looked fine before."

"Looked is past tense. That means I don't look fine
now."
"Stop complaining!"
You grabbed my wrists, forcing them to stay above my
head,
aggressively the sweater flew to the ground.
My wrists marked with your strength,
an evil tint simmered in your eyes,
the sweater flying out the window.

"Don't test me."

(I never wore sweaters again.)

If only I didn't walk into my room.
It was my house; it was *my* house.
You didn't have the right
to be on the property without my permission.

You never came into my house without me.
But chivalry worked on anyone these days.
The door to my room was ajar,
I never left my room unlocked.

And you were the only one with the spare key.

The faint cherry perfume, all too familiar,
burned my nose as I inhaled and pushed the door
further.

The air escaped my lungs, knees pulled by gravity to the
floor,
your face buried in her hair.

You were no longer holding me in your arms.
But her, *my* best friend, in *my* bed.
The gold chain I once thought you'd give to me
around her neck, your initial clearly imprinted,
and you two weren't "just friends" anymore.

I slammed my door.

"Never trust the nice ones"

You weren't a nice one in the end.

Period

3

High school relationships didn't last

I hated this warning because it wasn't the case for my parents,
it wasn't the case for my aunts and uncles,
it wasn't the case for my family.

So why was I the first?

High school relationships *did* last,
but maybe that's because they chose the right ones.

How could I have chosen so wrong…

Lust or love

Neither.

But it was lonely.

I loved the loneliness
but I loved how it was right now.

I should've known better

But why didn't I trust my gut?

Different

I'm not the same person
who fell in love with you.
I'm not the same person
who thought the world
wouldn't hurt her if she
stayed with her soulmate.

How naïve of me to think we could've been soulmates...

We were never the same,
we never would be.
I should've known my values
were flattened and pressed
to fit the idealised world
you thrived in.

The world you loved and desired
held promises of fame and beauty
in all forms, shapes and sizes.
But these came with the consequence
of losing oneself and never being whole again.

Your manipulated story
flashed brightly from your fingertips
each time you captured another scripted memory.
Your cards cleared daily,
but mine stuffed to the brim,
remembering each word and action

so you captured the essence of beauty.

Scripted beauty lied to young girls
telling them how everything could be
the way it was if they looked pretty or
found success in the industry to
turn young hearts into hardened scars.

We were different.
and different was good.

But to you,
different was everything against you,
and that was no way to live.

At least not for us.

Ticking time bomb

I should've seen your anger bubbling ages ago.
The anger that told me my deepest fears were true.
You were a ticking time bomb.
The trauma you pent up
overflowed the gates,
pouring down my face
like careless whispers of
"true love".

We weren't meant to make it out alive.

Tears

The edges of our photographs separated us now.
Not only pictures in little rectangles
across the pages of a grade book,
but a wall between us that magically grew wider
when,

"I'm done,"

was spoken.

Forever broke between us

Like the tears in our pictures
from age, love and neglect.

Negative space

You were tough to be around on your best days,
and your worst days were nightmares in daylight.

You took over my mind every minute of every hour,
making me question if I did you wrong.

You criticised my every move and every word
like you were afraid I'd slip up and damage you.

I stared at your photo and the negative space,
then at mine and the negative space.

No wonder I hated myself.
You ensured I always would.

Changing seasons

Were hard to go through,
but you were the filter
I needed to remove
when this winter passed.

Damaged photographs

Tear-stained, ripped, crumpled.
Photographs of us, of me, of you —
photographs that told our story.

But like all stories,
it was just fiction.

Leaving you behind

Was the best decision I made for me.
I was free from the toxicity, the pollution, the poison
that confined me to the mirrored walls of myself,
of expectations, of society, of you.

I no longer fit into the puzzle you crafted.
I never fit into you.

You could've tried to contain
and squeeze me in as the missing piece.

But you and I both knew there wasn't a missing piece.

There was only an extra piece of the puzzle,
one that came out of nowhere,
had no home, had no room in any box.

This puzzle piece didn't find a home
with the jigsaw that pretended to want her.
This piece needed to find a home
developed from pure love,
not the falsities that kept her in the dark
to hide away from scrutiny,
chipping or scarring.

This puzzle piece needed more than
what your jigsaw offered.

Your jigsaw was too small
to hold all the intricacies that made
one fun and challenging.

So she found her jigsaw
and fit right in.

Leaving you behind.
Signed,
the new me.

Why did I let you in

I might've been young, but I wasn't foolish.
To you I was dumb, naïve, easy,
and I proved you right.

But now I was proving to myself
that I am beautiful.

Because I am.

And I'm learning that love didn't
only come from you.

Pretending

that everything was fine – overrated.
I'm done pretending,
should've been after the night
you told me I was beautiful when I didn't eat all day,
when I had my makeup done professionally,
when my lungs screamed from overexerting at the gym.

Pretending only turned me into someone
I wasn't meant to be.
I wasn't going to fit in
because I'm unique.
I'd never adapt to your life,
one filled with models, luxury,
front-page stories,
perfectly polished and posed photographs.

Your life wasn't mine,
nor could it ever be.

It wasn't a part of me.

My dreams held nothing
but to heal from your destruction.
Life to me was more than the negatives
and I aspired to change the focal point
you pressed into my mind.

You took away my life the moment I met you.

And I was going to take it back.

Step 1 was removing you from the picture.
Step 2 was burning you to ashes.
Step 3 was finding me.

I've destroyed your dreams
trying to find mine that you faded.
I didn't care if you were hurting,
tapping a credit card on the reader
that declined from my control.

You weren't taking the photos now.

Our pictures sung in the fireplace,
the flames losing their recordings of us
from "happier times" that were never the case.
The old cute moments I cherished
turned dark and harsh, the grayscale
bleeding through the image
and slicing apart the perfect shot.

I desired a new take.

And this time, I was taking the photos alone.

I should've stopped pretending...

Where would I have been

If I didn't fall for you back then?
Would I be in this situation,
would I doubt myself,
would I believe I was beautiful?
If I didn't fall for you back then,
would I be happier,
would I remember what love was,
would I breathe without struggle?

If I didn't fall for you back then,
where would I have been?

What-if moments stopped

I didn't need to erase our history from existence
to know that you would've done this if we were friends.
That's how it all started.

Friends to lovers.

I knew who I was dealing with four years ago
and I still let myself fall into the trap.
But anyone who's advanced was a beginner first.

And you taught me the basics without intention.

Falsified reality

You saw me for someone you wanted to be with,
not for who I was and who I wanted to become.
It was like wanting a trophy, finally winning it,
and shoving it to the back of the shelf,
never to look at again
but always on display.

Did you like the idea of me?

I was the one you could mould,
transform and manipulate
like a marionette, painted beautifully
to agree with everything you asked for.

You had the world in your hands.
Your calculated plans, perfected moments,
scripted vows that were flawless.

But there was always a flaw.

Me.

The flaw you tried to assimilate but couldn't.
I wasn't meant for you, and you weren't meant for me.
Even if "happy ever after" sounded perfect,
the last four years should've been everything
but the perfect jigsaw I gave you as a gift.

Eventually, you realised too.

The perfect jigsaw didn't include me.
And your "pretty" marionette,
                  well,

                            she died too.

Marionette strings
            ripped;

                    puzzles
                      chipped.

Meaningless

Was I to you.

I was never going to be
the ideal girl you wanted.
I'd never measure up to
the supermodels you followed.
I could've gotten surgery,
manipulated my true form,
changed every little thing about me.

But that wasn't me.

I never wanted to grow up
in a society where "beautiful"
was everything that wasn't me.

It was being taught that you were pretty,
but you could never love models
if you weren't like them.

It was being taught that you were smart,
but no one wanted the brains
without the beauty.

It was being taught that I
was insignificant as an individual
if I didn't become someone's copy.

So what if I was meaningless to you?

Maybe being meaningless was better
than broken and tormented by you?

This shouldn't be

How we lived our lives on this planet,
how we saw ourselves in a crowd of others,
how we told ourselves we weren't beautiful.

Beautiful wasn't one size fits all.

And I know I'm not the only one.

I needed to fall in love

Not with you, not with him, not with her

but with me.

Period

4

Filtered

Everything was nowadays,
but if we went back to the past,
it wasn't any different.

Sure, it wasn't as advanced
but filters still existed.
Whether detailed makeup
that completely altered one's appearance
or changing their physique to fit in with
societal standards when unnecessary.

Everyone changed their appearance
because nothing was forever perfect
or beautiful in time.

It lasted for an era,
short or long,
it was just an era.

We're filtered to be
beautiful, smart, quirky.
Filters extended more than looks.
But the filters of appearance
ripped our cardboard pieces
quicker than water damaged
the completed jigsaw.

Filters only altered perception

but ingrained in our conscience
that "beautiful" isn't us
but always someone else.

Someone we believed we were.

Fragile

My heart shattered knowing I wasn't alone,
but I hated knowing that this was too common.
No one should've felt this way.

Everyone was beautiful in their own way.

And I hated knowing it was a curse
that we would never see past.

I escaped you physically,
but you were forever around
mentally and emotionally, dictating
my next moves, the next thing I wore,
the way I chose to do my makeup.

I never expected that one day
we would end things between us.
But now, I'm glad we did
because there was nothing worse
than holding onto the negative hope
in life when I needed to spread my arms

and break the mirror.

Fragile hearts broke
day in and day out.
The tears and shards stuck
like frozen icicles trapped

within the confines of love
that never got reciprocated.

The curse of beauty blinded
the ones we thought, hoped,
prayed were the right ones.

But those prayers weren't answered,
and left were fragile hearts
damaged from trust.

I'm not alone

Comforting but disturbing.
Fearless but fearful.
Alone but together.

I'm not alone
and I'm building my empire
of the next generation to inspire you.

Vulnerability wasn't weak

Why did we deem it a weakness
when to admit our secrets and fears
in a world that was constantly evolving,
proved our adaptability to change with it
at the speed of light,
innovating ways to alter our reality?

Vulnerability isn't weak
and never should've been.
It wasn't a reason to stop speaking up,
to stop sharing the truth, to stop expressing

the truths of what we should've said
from the start of time.

Expectation and reality

They almost never coincided.

Authentic

Was better than fake.

Mindset was everything

That's what they always said when you were young
but they weren't joking when life wasn't seen
through rose-coloured glasses.

I needed a fresh perspective.
One that didn't tell me
I was too fat,
my stomach hung out over the waistband,
my arms too chubby
and my legs not straight and tall.

I might not be perfect in their eyes.
But I was perfect for me.
I was *always* perfect for me.

Especially before the diets,
the insane health culture
that became a toxic race to
the next smaller ten.

I was forever perfect in my skin.

I needed a fresh perspective,
one that wasn't tainted by society,
by family, by friends, by anyone.

But that wasn't realistic in today's world.

A fresh perspective today wasn't simple
but it was the thought that counted.
The effort to ignore certain comments,
to remember I am worthy,
living my life the way I wanted.

I would change my thoughts.

I wanted to live a life
where I could toss away
any ill comments about myself
from others and my inner critic
because I didn't need to believe them.

I didn't need them to rule my life.

     I was always pretty.

I was always worthy.
I was always perfect.

I was always beautiful.

The world didn't need to think that.
Society could throw negativity at me
but I was going to be comfortable,
comfortable in my skin.

I would wear the clothes I wanted to,
I would wear no makeup on the days I wanted to,
I would embrace my true, authentic self

the way I should've a long time ago.

Authentic was better than fake
and faking it only got me nowhere.

I was a new person in their eyes,
but I was myself in a world
that tried to change me.

Unfiltered

In a world of filters,
life wasn't perfect and picturesque.
In a world of editing,
our flaws weren't altered to hide their existence.
In a world of influence,
we weren't made to be alike, carbon copies.

We are uniquely beautiful.

I finally took off the filters and saw what I should've all
those years ago.

Not for anyone else — I did it for me

It never should've been.
I shouldn't have changed myself
to become the girl you dreamed of.
I wasn't even the girl you wanted in the end.
You wanted my best friend.

You: Never loved her,
glad it's over now.
We're finally free princess!

Best friend: Low-key I kind of miss her.
But she was annoying to deal with every day.
Probably for the best.

You: I guess I miss her money.
But her attitude was more than
I ever took out of her account.

I'm okay with it now.

They could say what they wanted
but I wouldn't let it bother me.
Their comments only reminded me
of the past I needed to leave behind.

I knew I'd never be everyone's cup of tea

but it's easier to move on when the drama
passed the boiling point and the bitterness
fades.

I'd admit she was pretty, smart, charismatic,
your total package.
Any guy would be lucky to spend his life with her.

But I didn't feel jealous of her looks,
her brain, her personality, her easy charm.

Not anymore.

Not when I was working towards a happier life.

But I also didn't want to live the rest of my life,
with or without you,
thinking I wasn't beautiful.

Because it wasn't as simple
as flicking my wrist and
waving a magic wand to
hide the past from my reality.

Beautiful wasn't attainable
in the puzzled, scrutinising eyes of society.
But beautiful to my standards
was enough.

And that's all it had to be.

Enough for me.

Because I'm the only one
who needed to love herself
for who she truly was.

I finally knew what beautiful was.

And I won't ever let you ruin that for me again.

True to myself
And never forgetting myself for them.

New reflections

Goodbye to the old me,
the girl who lied to everyone to stay perfect,
the girl who trusted other opinions over her own,
the girl who listened to everyone but herself,
the girl who wasn't me.
Goodbye.

Thank you for reading *Like Me, For Me*! If you enjoyed the book, I would be beyond grateful if you left a review on any platform of your choice.

Reviews are so beneficial for authors and each one helps!

Love always,
Isabella

Instagram:
@isabellajuanitalyn

YouTube:
www.youtube.com/@isabellajuanitalyn

Acknowledgements

I am honestly at a loss for words as I write this. This concept has been forever near and dear to my heart. I have always wanted to bring it to life but never had the chance until now.

And I'm glad I did it justice.

This collection is one my younger self would've loved. She needed this book more than she knew and I'm so happy I finally fulfilled that small part of her dream.

This book would never be where it's at today without my wonderful readers, editors, illustrator and close ones.

I kept this story a secret from you, and I hope you can forgive me.

Thank you to my wonderful critique partner and proofreader Talia and beta readers Olivia and Amber. You were all so supportive and excited for this collection when I lost hope. You helped me get through the hard days and I'm so glad we're finally at the end of this story's journey. The feedback is forever appreciated, and I love the attention to detail you always give to my stories.

I am so thankful for such honest and compassionate friends who will go above and beyond to help me achieve my dreams!

Thank you for never doubting me or this story. You guys are literally the best friends a girl could ask for!

Thank you to Krystal for the wonderful illustration. I know my draft was something traumatic that you might never recover from, but your patience and dedication to this story is forever appreciated and I could never have brought this design to life without your amazing artistic talents.

Thank you to Mimi for helping me remember this story and all its potential. I can't imagine what this year would've been like without this collection.

And finally, thank you to you, the reader, for showing this book so much love and adoration. I am continuously overjoyed by the constant happiness I receive. You deserve the world!

Love Always,
Isabella

Isabella Juanita Lyn is an author, poet, and digital creator. With a focus on love and heartbreak, her books contain heart-wrenching emotions to help others find themselves. She strives to aspire others to follow their dreams and most importantly, stand up for themselves and their beliefs. Besides writing, reading, and creating content, Isabella is obsessed with piglets and bunnies, learning random things in the world of Economics and Mathematics, and finding joy in life's little things.

9 780648 649083